D0475549

NO LONGER PROPERTY OF
SEATTLE PUBLIC LIBRARY

Dedicated, with apologies, to my cat Beatrix,
who would never chase a mouse—or would she?
—D.H.

To my daughter and her wife
—P.O.Z.

Text copyright © 2023 by Deborah Hopkinson
Jacket art and interior illustrations copyright © 2023 by Paul O. Zelinsky

All rights reserved. Published in the United States by Anne Schwartz Books, an imprint of Random House
Children's Books, a division of Penguin Random House LLC, New York.

Anne Schwartz Books and the colophon are trademarks of Penguin Random House LLC.

Visit us on the Web! rhcbooks.com

Educators and librarians, for a variety of teaching tools, visit us at RHTeachersLibrarians.com

Library of Congress Cataloging-in-Publication Data is available upon request.
ISBN 978-0-593-48003-8 (trade) — ISBN 978-0-593-48004-5 (lib. bdg.) — ISBN 978-0-593-48005-2 (ebook)

The text of this book is set in 12.5-point Cotford Text.
The illustrations were drawn piecemeal in ink, then scanned and assembled,
with color and more lines added digitally.
Book design by Nicole de las Heras

MANUFACTURED IN CHINA
10 9 8 7 6 5 4 3 2 1
First Edition

Random House Children's Books supports the First Amendment and celebrates the right to read.

Penguin Random House LLC supports copyright. Copyright fuels creativity, encourages diverse voices,
promotes free speech, and creates a vibrant culture. Thank you for buying an authorized edition
of this book and for complying with copyright laws by not reproducing, scanning,
or distributing any part in any form without permission. You are supporting writers
and allowing Penguin Random House to publish books for every reader.

Cinderella and a Mouse Called Fred

written by

DEBORAH HOPKINSON

illustrated by

PAUL O. ZELINSKY

a·s·b

anne schwartz books

Once upon a time, there was a small gray mouse who lived in a pumpkin patch. It was a quiet life—until the night a stranger appeared.

"Where's the moon when I need it?"
she grumbled. "I'll never find a pumpkin
for Cinderella."

Cinderella? The mouse's ears shot up.
Why, he *knew* Cinderella, or Ella,
as her friends called her.

She'd surprised him one
day as he sat scratching his
ears behind an especially
plump pumpkin.

Ella had been carrying a shovel, but
she hadn't tried to squash him. Instead,
she smiled and said, "Hello, little friend.
What kind and curious eyes you have. You
look like a Fred."

*Such a distinguished name. I like
it!* the mouse decided. He'd shot her a
glance that he hoped was kind, curious,
and fabulously Fred-ish.

"Thanks for keeping watch over my pumpkin, Fred. I plan to win a prize with it, so no nibbling, please," Ella had said, then added, "And better not come near the house. My wicked stepmother and stepsisters don't like mice—or me, either, even though I do all the chores. Plus, there's a *cat*."

Fred had been sorry
to hear this nice human
had to put up with such
a mean family—to say
nothing of a cat.

Now he asked the stranger, who seemed able to converse quite easily in Rodent, "Why do you want a pumpkin for Ella?"

"Because I'm her fairy godmother, *obviously*," she said in a huff. "So is there a pumpkin in this tangled mess or not?"

Temper, temper, Fred thought. He wondered if all fairy godmothers were grouchy. But since he was indeed kind, all he said was, "There's a nice one right here."

And the fairy godmother picked the pumpkin—just like that.

Fred winced. It would never win a prize now.

Then she turned to him.
"I guess you'll do, mouse,"
she said, and tapped him
with her wand.

Suddenly, Fred felt himself tumbling about,

like a little lost leaf in a storm.

The next thing he knew, he had a long silver mane

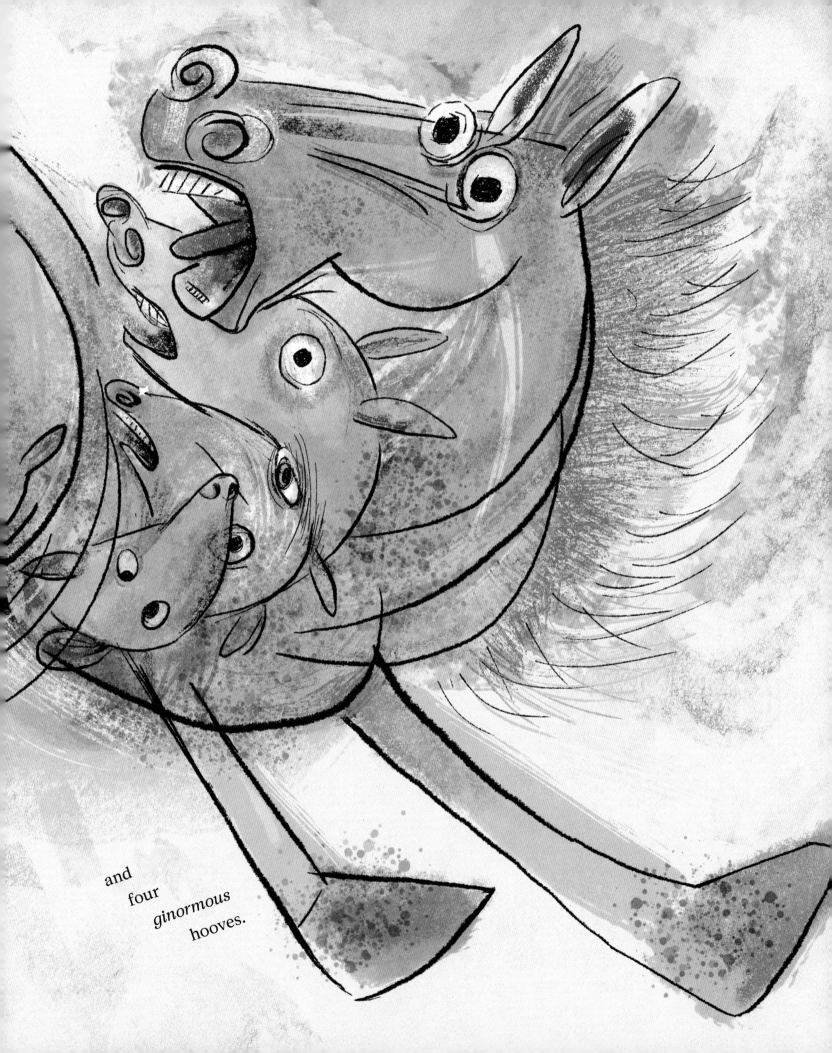

and
four
ginormous
hooves.

Goodness! He was attached to some sort of gaudy orange contraption. And there was Ella, all dressed up and fancy.

"No time to get a coachman, dearie," the fairy godmother was saying. "You'll have to drive."

"It's all good," said Ella. But as she was climbing up, she stumbled. "Seriously? Glass high heels?"

"Be home before the last stroke of midnight, or your steed and coach will turn back into that scrawny little mouse and the pumpkin," the fairy godmother warned. "And your gown will become your sooty old Cinderella rags again."

Oh, have a heart. Let her keep the dress! Fred tried to squeak. It came out like a neigh.

The fairy godmother gave him a rude smack on his flank. "Walk on."

And off they went, just like in the fairy tale.

Fred wasn't sure how he felt about being a horse. His ears still itched terribly, and so far as he could figure, there was no way to get a hoof anywhere near them.

When they arrived at the palace, Ella clambered down and scratched Fred's ears. Ah, relief!

"You have kind and curious eyes," she told him. "I bet you're Fred, the mouse who keeps watch over my best pumpkin."

Fred supposed horses were used to standing around, but *whoa,* talk about boring! He tried amusing himself by humming along with the music drifting out of the palace. Some of the tunes were quite catchy, and he made up a little dance to help pass the time.

It occurred to Fred that if he were still a mouse, he could have scored a ringside seat to the entire extravaganza, including the cheese platters.

Instead, he had to imagine Ella twirling with the prince, whoever that was.

At last Ella appeared, hobbling back in only one glass slipper. After a few hobbles, she yanked it off and threw it against a lamppost.

Just looking at the shards made Fred's hooves hurt.

"What a disaster!" Ella cried as she climbed into the coach. "My feet are killing me. And that so-called prince? When I told him I loved to garden, he sniffed and said, 'I abhor dirt.'"

Bummer, Fred thought. He wondered if there was a way to give the fairy godmother a one-star rating.

Ella flicked the reins. "Home, Fred!" And off he trotted.

When Fred heard the first chime of the town clock
strike midnight, he broke into a gallop.
But wait! What were those tiny scurrying things?
A family of mice! Even worse, Fred recognized them.

"Watch out, Auntie Em," he neighed. "Run for your lives, cousins!"
Just as Fred was about to trample baby Wilhelm . . .

. . . the clock chimed the last stroke of twelve. Again, Fred was tumbled about in that ghastly manner.

When he opened his eyes, his ears itched. He scratched them with his mouse paw. *Ahhhh!*

Once Wilhelm had scampered safely away, Fred spun around to check on Ella.

She was picking up pieces of smushed pumpkin
and sticking seeds into her pocket.

"That was . . . unusual,"
she said. She gave Fred a
seed to nibble, then tucked
him into her other pocket
and set off for home.

The next morning,
Ella and Fred watched the royal coach
arrive. Ella's stepmother and stepsisters
bustled out to greet the prince, who appeared
to be looking for the owner of the glass
slipper he held.

"I can't wait to see this," Ella said.

Well, you can guess what happened next. The first stepsister couldn't get her big toe in. The second couldn't even get her little toe in. They bickered. They berated the slipper. The stepmother yowled. The cat joined in. The prince's face scrunched up. Finally, Fred simply had to cover his eyes.

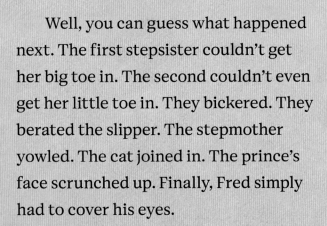

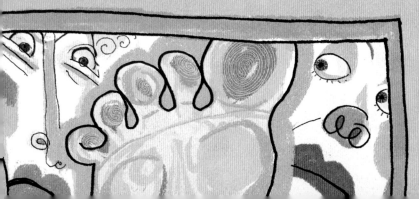

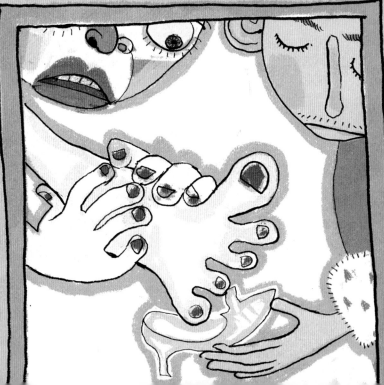

As the coach rolled past them, Ella hid behind some Brussels sprouts. "I'd say he's in for a wild goose chase," she remarked, then laughed. "I'll find my own destiny, thank you very much."

I guess that's that, thought Fred.

But as it turned out, it was just the beginning. . . .

The next spring, Ella planted the pumpkin seeds she'd saved. One grew into a spectacular pumpkin, like nothing anyone had ever seen.

"What shall we call it?" she asked Fred one day. He secretly hoped Ella would name it after him: the Fred pumpkin. And well she might have, but fate intervened.

That fall, Ella and her pumpkin won a blue ribbon at the fair.

They beat out a young farmer, who fell madly in love with Ella, just as she was. And Ella loved her right back.

Ella and the farmer got married and moved
to a small farm, where Fred kept careful watch
over their magical, magnificent pumpkins.
It was a fairy-tale ending after all.

And that, dear reader,
is the story of how
fairytale pumpkins got their name.

ABOUT FAIRYTALE PUMPKINS

The tale of Cinderella has been told, in one form or another, for centuries. This retelling has its roots in the version written in 1697 by French author Charles Perrault. Perrault's story includes a fairy godmother, glass slippers, and a pumpkin coach pulled by six beautiful, mouse-colored gray horses (formerly mice, of course).

Like the fairy tale, pumpkins have been around for a long time—more than five thousand years. Some pumpkins are tiny. Others grow to giants, weighing as much as two thousand pounds. (Good thing Fred didn't have to pull one of those.)

Pumpkins come in many colors, including orange, white, and even blue-green. People who grow and develop different pumpkin varieties, called hybrids, sometimes give them fun names, such as Casper, Bumpkin, Munchkin, Baby Boo, Warty Goblin, Jack Be Little, or Peanut.

Fairytale pumpkins are a variety of French heirloom pumpkins officially known as Musquee de Provence. While I'm not quite sure how they got their nickname, it's likely because early illustrators of Charles Perrault's "Cinderella" based their pumpkin coaches on these deep-lobed beauties. A different variety is said to have inspired Cinderella's coach in the 1950 Disney film; it's known as a Cinderella pumpkin.

I can't wait to plant fairytale pumpkins in my garden. And who knows? Maybe this version of the tale will inspire a new pumpkin: the Fred pumpkin.

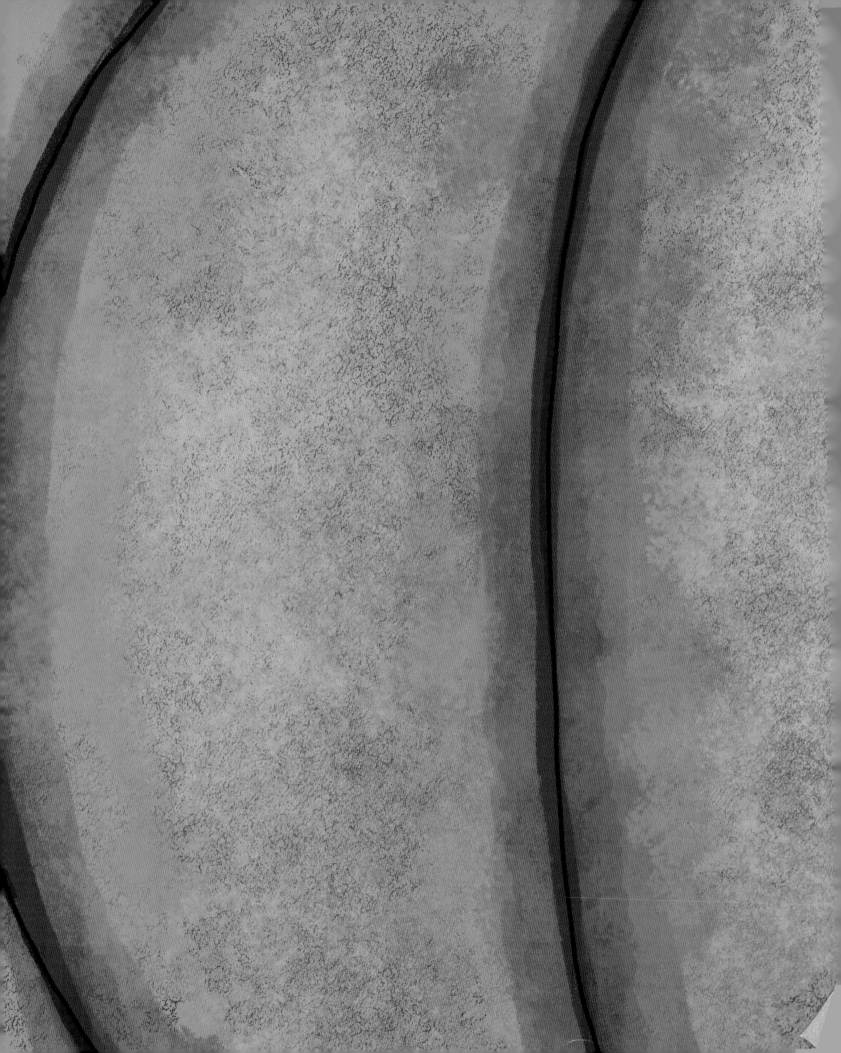